ANDREW

*Poor Andrew McAndrew didn't see the nail
and he rode right over it.*

# ANDREW MCANDREW

Written by
BERNARD MAC LAVERTY

Illustrated by
DUNCAN SMITH

WALKER BOOKS
LONDON

*For Judith*

"Andrew McAndrew and the Red Bike" and
"Andrew McAndrew and the Wheels" first published in
*Wide Range Reader: Green Book 1* by
Schonell and Flowerdew, Oliver & Boyd Ltd 1985

First published 1988 by
Walker Books Ltd, 87 Vauxhall Walk
London SE11 5HJ

Paperback edition published 1989

First printed 1988
Printed in Great Britain by
Richard Clay Ltd, Bungay, Suffolk

British Library Cataloguing in Publication Data
Mac Laverty, Bernard
Andrew McAndrew.
I. Title  II. Smith, Duncan, *1957–*
823'.914[J]    PZ7

ISBN 0-7445-0822-3
ISBN 0-7445-0830-4 Pbk

# CONTENTS

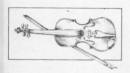

*"Andrew McAndrew, what would you like?*
*All I want is a little red bike."*

# ANDREW McANDREW
# AND THE
# RED BIKE

The thing Andrew McAndrew wanted most was a bike. Each night, before he went to sleep, he said a little rhyme to himself, which was a kind of wish.

*"Andrew McAndrew, what would
   you like?
All I want is a little red bike."*

But he never thought that anybody heard him. On the morning of his birthday, his mother woke him up.

"Happy birthday, Andrew McAndrew," she said and gave him a hug. "Come downstairs for your birthday present."

Andrew McAndrew ran downstairs and in the hall he saw something all wrapped in brown paper. He tore off the paper.

"What is it? What is it?" he said.

When he tore off the last of the paper his mother said, "Now you know what it is."

It was a bike – a *red* bike just like the one he had always wanted. It had a white pump to pump up the tyres. And when the wheels went round they made a loud whirring noise. But best of all it had a silvery bell which Andrew McAndrew rang and rang. Then he thanked his mum and dad and went out to ride his bicycle without having any breakfast.

Now Andrew McAndrew's grandad lived just down the street. The boy loved his grandad and wanted to show his new bike to him before he did anything else.

There was a sharp nail on the road outside

his grandad's gate. Poor Andrew McAndrew didn't see it and he rode right over it. Suddenly there was a noise – *pssssss* – and all the air hissed out of his front tyre.

"Oh me, oh my, oh me!" said Andrew McAndrew. He wanted to cry when he saw his tyre was flat. Instead of crying, he wished again with his rhyme.

*"Andrew McAndrew, what would you like?*
*Somebody big to fix my new bike."*

Just then his grandad came out of the gate. He had a white moustache and he smoked a pipe and he cut up his tobacco with a little knife.

"Happy birthday, Andrew McAndrew," he said. Andrew McAndrew showed his grandad his bike and then told him about the burst tyre. He wanted to cry again.

His grandad patted him on the head and said, "Don't worry, I'll fix it for you."

His grandad could fix anything. He got a little box from the kitchen and two spoons and a basin full of water. He took off the tyre and showed Andrew McAndrew the little hole the nail had made. He cut a small patch from a piece of old rubber with his tobacco knife and stuck it over the hole.

"There we are," he said. "Now all we have to do is pump it up again."

He began to pump up the tyre with the new white pump. Andrew McAndrew saw the tyre get fat again. His grandad pumped until the tyre was like new.

"That's it fixed!"

Now Andrew McAndrew did not feel like crying. He was happy again. He showed off the brakes to his grandad. He spun the wheels. And best of all he let him listen to the silvery bell which made a grand noise.

"Goodbye!" shouted Andrew McAndrew. And he rode off down the road again. As he rode along he said a little rhyme.

*"Andrew McAndrew, what would
   you like?
All my friends to see my new bike."*

And he went to call for all his friends to show them the newness of his red bike.

*Andrew McAndrew's grandad had a shed full of old tins of paint in all the colours of the rainbow.*

# ANDREW McANDREW
## AND THE
## BELLS

Andrew McAndrew loved to visit his grandad. His house was filled with good things to play with. But they weren't toys. He had a button box full of old buttons, a tin full of nails and screws and bolts and a shed full of old tins of paint in all the colours of the rainbow. And he had lots of interesting ornaments. Best of all these ornaments Andrew McAndrew liked his grandad's shiny bells which sat on the mantelpiece. There were three of them; the big one sounded a bit like DONG-DONG, the middle-sized one sounded a bit like DENG-ELANG and the little one a bit like *ding-aling-aling*.

One day in the spring, when Andrew McAndrew was visiting, his grandad said, "Well, Andrew McAndrew, did you notice the flowers in the garden?"

"Yes, Grandad. What's your favourite?"

"Oh, I like bluebells," he said. "Bluebells are my favourite." And then his grandad went to sleep in his armchair and snored. He was always falling asleep. Andrew McAndrew said a little rhyme to himself.

*"Andrew McAndrew, what is there to do?*
*Paint Grandad's bells a nice shade of*
*blue."*

So he left his grandad sleeping and went out to the shed. It had a door which squeaked when he opened it. Andrew McAndrew looked at all the old tins of paint. There was red and there was yellow.

There was green and there was white. And there was *blue*. He found a paintbrush and took the blue paint into the house. He said another little rhyme.

*"Andrew McAndrew, don't make a mistake.*
*Ring the bell and Grandad will wake."*

So very quietly he took down the biggest bell and painted it blue. SLIP-SLOP, SLIP-SLOP went the brush over the bell. He held it by the little bit that hangs down inside so that it wouldn't make any noise. Then he painted the middle-sized bell, SLEP-SLAP, SLEP-SLAP, until it was blue all over. Then last of all he did the wee-est bell, *slip-slip, slippity*. He put them all back on the mantelpiece. But they weren't shiny any more, they were blue. And still his grandad snored. Andrew McAndrew said another little rhyme.

*"Andrew McAndrew, get Grandad awake.*
*But how will I do it? Give him a shake."*

He gave his grandad a shake and he woke up.

"Uhhhgggmumumum. What is it?"

"I've made your favourites."

"What's that, eh?"

"Blue bells," said Andrew McAndrew, and he showed him the bells on the mantelpiece.

"Andrew McAndrew! You're a divil! What sort of boy are you, eh?"

He sounded angry.

"I thought you liked them," said Andrew McAndrew.

*"Andrew McAndrew! You're a divil!
What sort of boy are you, eh?"*

"I like bluebell *flowers*, not blue bells. Bells don't work with blue paint on them. Listen."

And he lifted up each bell and jiggled it. The big one sounded like PONK-PONK, the middle one sounded like DEB-DIB and the wee-est one sounded like *tip-tip*.

Andrew McAndrew wanted to cry. He said to himself:

*"Andrew McAndrew, before I count ten
Please make the bells shiny again."*

But his grandad said, "Don't worry, I can fix it. The paint's not dry yet."

And he went out to his shed with the squeaky door and brought in a bottle of stuff which would take the paint off. *Slip-slop, slip-slop, slip-slop*. He brushed it all over the bells and wiped them clean with a cloth until they were nice and shiny – just like they were before.

"Now listen to the difference," said his grandad. He picked up the biggest bell and it made a noise like DONG-DONG. Then he picked up the middle-sized bell and it made a sound like DENG-ELANG, and he picked up the wee-est bell and it rang like *ding-aling-aling*.

"Now, Andrew McAndrew, we'll go out to the shed and put this tin of blue paint away. And while we're out there I'll show you some *real* bluebells."

And his grandad took him to the garden and showed him the buttercups and the daisies and the *real* bluebells.

*Andrew liked to play a game of running very fast to the next lamp-post, then going very slow,*

# ANDREW McANDREW
# AND THE
# RECORD PLAYER

One day Andrew McAndrew went down the street to visit his grandad. When he was walking by himself Andrew liked to play a game of running very fast to the next lamp-post, then going very slow to get his breath back. He would run a lamp-post and walk a lamp-post. When he went into his grandad's house he had just run a lamp-post and he was panting and puffing.

"Hello, Andrew McAndrew. What have you been chasing?"

"Lamp-posts," said Andrew. His grandad was bending over a funny machine and poking at it. Andrew asked him what it was.

"It's a record player – for making music."

"Can I hear some?" said Andrew, doing small jumps in the middle of the floor.

"Just as soon as I get this plug wired up."

Whenever Andrew McAndrew wanted anything badly he always made up a little rhyme and very often he got his wish. He made up one now.

*"I wish, I wish with all my might
I could play music until tonight."*

His grandad set down his screwdriver and said, "That's it, Andrew McAndrew, we're ready to go."

He lifted a record and put it on the turntable but then he stopped.

"Let's get some of the little girls and boys from the street. I'm sure they'd like to hear some music as well. And we can have some lemonade and biscuits while we're listening."

Andrew's grandad left the room, but before he went out the door he said, "Don't you touch anything, Andrew McAndrew, do you hear me?"

"No, Grandad."

Andrew McAndrew sat on his own looking at the record player. Everything was very quiet – so quiet he could hear the birds chirping outside in the street. He wanted to hear the music. His grandad was taking *ages* to find the other children. Andrew looked at some of the switches and the little arm with the needle that played the record. He said a little rhyme to himself.

*"Grandad is taking far too long,*
*So I, myself, will play the song."*

There was a tiny lever with numbers written beside it. He moved it, *click*, but nothing happened. He switched a switch, *clunk*, and the turntable went round and round. He lifted the little arm with its needle and set it on the record.

*Diddle-diddle-middly-middly-diddly-middly.*

That didn't sound right. Andrew McAndrew moved the lever with the numbers on it and tried again.

POMP-BOMP-WOOA-WOAH-BOMP.

That didn't sound right either. He switched the machine off and began to bite his nails.

"I've broken it," he thought, "and my grandad will be mad and give me a row."

"I've broken it," he thought, "and my grandad
will be mad and give me a row."

He made up another rhyme.

*"Andrew McAndrew, alas and alack!*
*Let the player be fixed before he*
*comes back."*

But his rhymes didn't work all the time.
His grandad came in with lots of children.
They were all excited and giggling, wanting
to hear the music. Andrew's grandad gave
them all lemonade and biscuits and asked
them to sit on the floor and be quiet. They
were all silent as they watched him turn on
the record player.

"Listen to this lovely music," he said and
put the needle on the record.

POMP-BOMP-WOOA-WOAH-BOMP.

"What . . . what?" Grandad's face turned

red. The children all laughed and rolled on the floor and giggled and kicked their legs in the air. Some choked on their biscuits and spilled their lemonade.

"Who's been fiddling with my record player?" said Grandad. He sounded very angry.

Andrew McAndrew said, "It was me, Grandad. All I did was touch that . . ." and he moved the tiny lever again.

*Diddle-diddle-middly-middly-diddly-middly.*

And the children all laughed so much that they fell down on the floor again.

"Stop it!" yelled Grandad. He took the needle off the record. "Don't worry, I can fix it," he said. "This wee lever is for making the record go fast or slow. You have to play it at the right speed. Andrew McAn-

*Grandad played the record at the right speed
and all the children danced around the room.*

drew, you're a divil!" But he winked at him and Andrew McAndrew knew that he wasn't cross any more. He heaved a sigh and made up another rhyme.

*"Grandad McAndrew has fixed*
  *the player,*
*That's the answer to my prayer."*

And Grandad played the record at the right speed and all the children danced around the room and the one who danced the most of all was Andrew McAndrew.

*"Hello, Andrew McAndrew."* Andrew smiled back
at him. They were smiley people.

# ANDREW McANDREW
## AND THE
## FIDDLE

One day Andrew McAndrew went to visit his grandad and when his grandad saw him he smiled – a big wide smile that made his white moustache turn upwards.

"Hello, Andrew McAndrew." Andrew smiled back at him. They were smiley people.

"Come in, laddie," Grandad said. "Some friends of mine are coming to see me and you can help me to get ready."

"Why are they coming?" asked Andrew.

"We're just going to have a wee party."

Andrew helped to set the cups on the table and to butter the bread for the sand-wiches.

"Now for the most important thing," said Grandad, and he reached up and opened a cupboard and took out his fiddle.

"You can't have a party without music. Music makes people smile. And at a party everybody should be smiling. But first of all I have to tune it."

He plucked one string. *Poink!*

"That's not right," he said and frowned. He twisted a little knob at the top of the fiddle and plucked the string.

*Poink – poink – pink – pink –
plink, plink, plink!*

"That's it now," he said and smiled. "Next!" and he plucked the next string. *Dunk!*

"That's not right," he said and frowned again. He twisted a different little knob at the top of the fiddle and plucked the string.

*Doink – doink – dink – dink –*
  *ding, ding, ding!*

"That's it now," he said and smiled. "Next."

And he tuned all the strings until they were right.

"Let's put it to the test, eh, Andrew?" and he took out his bow and began to play a tune on the fiddle.

Now when Andrew McAndrew wanted anything badly he said a little rhyme to himself and most of the time he got it. As he listened to his grandad playing he said to himself:

*"Andrew McAndrew, answer the riddle.*
*How can I play my grandad's fiddle?"*

33

His grandad stopped playing and put the fiddle in the cupboard and closed the door.

"I hope it doesn't go out of tune before the party," he said. Then Andrew's grandad's friends all began to arrive. Andrew looked out into the hallway and saw them all smiling. They were happy and all talking to each other. Andrew said another little rhyme to himself.

*"Andrew McAndrew, now's your chance,*
*Get the fiddle and play a dance."*

He climbed up on the chair, opened the cupboard door and took out the fiddle. He plinked the strings with his thumb. What a lovely sound, he thought. But the sound he had liked best was the sound his grandad had made when he turned the little knobs at the top. So Andrew plinked the strings and

*Andrew climbed up on the chair, opened the
cupboard door and took out the fiddle.*

*He turned all the little knobs at the
top and smiled at the sound.*

turned the little knobs at the top.

*Ding, ding – dink – dink – doink –* DUNK!

He turned all the little knobs at the top and smiled at the sound.

*Ping, ping – pink – pink –*
*poink – poink –* PUNK!

Then he heard his grandad coming so he quickly put the fiddle back in the cupboard.

"Everybody's here," said Grandad happily, "so we're going to have a little music." He reached into the cupboard and took his bow and fiddle.

Andrew and his grandad went into the other room and Andrew sat on the floor between all the grown-ups' feet. They were all smiling.

"I tuned this fiddle five minutes ago!" Grandad shouted. "Who's been fiddling with my fiddle?"

"Here's a nice little tune to start us off," said Grandad . . . and he lifted the bow . . . and began to play.

*Scritch – scratch – scrunk!*

It was awful. It was horrible. All the smiles disappeared. All the grown-ups were frowning. Their eyebrows were close together and their mouths were turned down at the corners. They were *not* happy. But the one who was frowning the most was Grandad. He looked angry.

"I tuned this fiddle five minutes ago!" he shouted. "Who's been fiddling with my fiddle?"

Andrew McAndrew knew it was him. He had done something wrong. He made a wish.

*"Andrew McAndrew, please make
   it right.
Please, please make all the strings tight."*

Then he said out loud, "Grandad, it was me. I didn't know. I just turned the knobs."

"Never mind," said his grandad. "I can fix it." And he turned the first knob a little.

*Poink – poink – pink – pink – plink,
   plink, plink!*

and the second and the third and the fourth until *all* the strings were right. Then he tried to play the tune again. He put the fiddle up to his shoulder . . . and he lifted up the bow . . . and began to play. This time it was great. All the grown-ups smiled. They raised their eyebrows high and the corners of their mouths turned up. They were happy and they tapped their feet to the music. And Andrew McAndrew was the happiest of them all. He said another little rhyme to himself.

*"Andrew McAndrew, things aren't so bad*
*With someone as good as my grandad."*

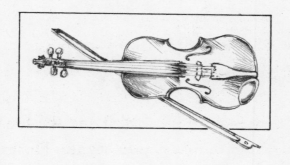

"I'm putting in a new sink,"
said Grandad. "The old one leaked."

# ANDREW McANDREW
# AND THE
# TAPS

One day when Andrew McAndrew was going down the street to visit his grandad, he heard a noise of hammering. Andrew was excited – his grandad must be fixing something. Maybe he could help him. He went into the house as quickly as he could. His grandad looked up when he saw him.

"Oh no. Hello, Andrew McAndrew." He was kneeling on the kitchen floor surrounded by tools and pipes and hammers and screwdrivers.

"This is great. What are you doing?" said Andrew.

"I'm putting in a new sink. The old one leaked."

"Can I help?"

"Yes, if you don't touch anything. Just sit there and watch." Andrew McAndrew sat on a stool and kicked his heels. Whenever he wanted anything badly he always made up a little rhyme and sometimes he got his wish. He made up one now.

*"I wish, I wish with all my might*
*I could help Grandad fix it right."*

Andrew's grandad, when he was working hard, liked to whistle a little tune to himself.

"Now we're nearly finished," he said. "Just three raps of the hammer," *rap-rap-rap*, "and three twists of the screwdriver," *ratchet-ratchet-ratchet*, "and three scrubs of the sandpaper," *shh-shh-shh*. "And now all I have to do is to put the tap tops on."

Andrew liked the sound of that. Tap tops. He said it to himself.

"Tap tops. The top of the taps. Tap tops." It sounded funny. His grandad lifted the tap tops and set them on.

"I need a special screwdriver for those. A tiny one to tighten them up. I think I've got one in the shed." His grandad went out to the shed whistling, but before he left he said, "Don't you touch anything, Andrew McAndrew, do you hear me?"

Andrew nodded his head. Today he would be very good. His grandad slammed the door and Andrew was left alone. He got off the stool and went over to the new sink. It was shiny stainless steel and the taps looked like silver. Andrew pulled the stool over to the sink and climbed up onto it. He said a little rhyme.

*Andrew's hands were slippery and the tap tops dropped with a clatter into the sink.*

*"One, two, three. Steady now, chaps,*
*Let's help Grandad with his taps."*

Andrew lifted the tap tops off and looked at them. One had a small blue circle on it and the other had a red circle on it. But Andrew's hands were slippery and the tap tops dropped with a clatter into the sink. Andrew bit his lip and said to himself:

*"Andrew McAndrew, you've made*
  *a mess.*
*Which one's which? You'll have*
  *to guess."*

And he put the tap tops on just as his grandad was coming through the back door whistling.

"This is the wee screwdriver I was look-ing for," he said.

His grandad began screwing on the tap tops. When he finished he cleared away all his tools and put them in the shed. He came back in and said, "Andrew McAndrew, that was very thirsty work. What would you say to a nice glass of orange juice?"

"Yes, please," said Andrew.

His grandad took a bottle of orange off the shelf and poured a little into each glass. He went to the new sink, turned on the tap and filled the glasses with water. He gave a glass to Andrew and took one himself.

"Cheers," said his grandad and drank his orange. "Urgshhh – euchhh – uggg!" He spat it out into the new sink. "It's hot orange juice. Has somebody been fiddling with my taps?" He sounded very angry. Andrew McAndrew bit his nails.

"It was me, Grandad. All I did was look at the tap tops."

"And put them back on the wrong taps. Don't worry. I can fix it."

He got his tools from the shed again, gave three raps of the hammer, *rap-rap-rap*, three twists of the screwdriver, *ratchet-ratchet-ratchet*, and three scrubs with the sandpaper, *shh-shh-shh*, and all was well again.

"The blue tap is for the *cold* water. The red tap is for the *hot* water. Remember that, Andrew McAndrew."

"Blue with cold and red with heat," said Andrew.

"Exactly," said his grandad as he threw the warm juice down the sink. He ran the cold tap so that it was very cold, then made two glasses of ice-cold juice. As they drank them Andrew made up another rhyme.

*"Andrew McAndrew, things aren't so bad
When you've got a really clever grandad."*

*There was a tall wooden clock in the corner with a white face and it ticked very slowly.*

# ANDREW McANDREW
## AND THE
## GRANDFATHER
## CLOCK

Andrew McAndrew sat in the front room of his own house. When he was alone Andrew always looked around him and saw as much as he could see. There was a tall wooden clock in the corner with a white face and it ticked very slowly.

*Tick!*
*Tick!*
*Tick!*

Suddenly the door opened and Andrew's grandad came in. Because he lived nearby he visited them every day.

"Hello, Andrew McAndrew!" he said.

*"I wind it up like this, by pulling one of the weights,"* said Grandad.

"What are you looking at?"

Andrew pointed. His grandad leaned his hand against the clock, which was taller than him.

"This is called a grandfather clock." He knocked on the wood with his knuckle. "Let me show you how it works."

He opened a small door in the clock's tummy and Andrew saw two big weights on a chain and a shiny thing which swung backwards and forwards, backwards and forwards.

"That's the pendulum. I wind it up like this, by pulling one of the weights." The chain made a rattling sound.

Andrew said one of his little rhymes.

*"Andrew McAndrew, wouldn't it*
*  be great,*
*If you could pull that great big weight."*

His grandad said to him, "The clock has to be right because do you know what night it is tonight?" Andrew shook his head. "It's Hogmanay."

"What's that?" asked Andrew.

"This is the last day of one year and at twelve o'clock, when both of the hands are pointing to the ceiling, it will be a new year. New Year's Day and everybody in the town makes a great hullaballo."

"What's a hullaballoo?" asked Andrew.

"It's noises and cheering. Bells ring and cars toot their horns and ships sound their sirens and trains blow their whistles. Oh, it's the greatest noise you've ever heard."

Andrew sat on the sofa and wished.

*"I wish, I wish with all my might*
*That I could stay up late tonight."*

He tried to imagine what all the noises would be like but he couldn't.

"If I wasn't in bed," said Andrew, "could I ring the bell on my wee red bike?"

"Oh surely, surely, Andrew McAndrew. That would be a great rackety noise."

"Can I stay up?"

His grandad went away to ask Andrew's mum and dad if he could stay up late. Andrew went over to the grandfather clock and opened the wee door and looked inside. He saw the weights and the shiny thing that went backwards and forwards. He pulled one of the weights but just then he heard his grandad coming back. He shut the wee door as quickly as he could.

"I'm afraid," said his grandad, "that everybody says you're too young to stay up."

So Andrew McAndrew had to go to bed at his usual time. He fell asleep thinking of all the excitement and noises he would miss. Then in the dark he woke up. He didn't know what time it was. Whenever he woke up in the dark he always shouted, "I wanna drinka watta!"

His mum came into his room. Andrew asked, "Is it next year yet?"

"No, but it will be soon. I suppose now that you're awake you can come down."

She lifted him and gave him a hug and carried him downstairs in his pyjamas. Everything was bright and shining. All the family were there including Grandad, and they were wearing party hats and drinking drinks. They were all standing round the grandfather clock and both hands were *nearly* pointing to the ceiling. Then Grandad said, "Shhh!"

"What's wrong, Grandad?"

"Shhh! I think the clock has stopped. It

can't be – I wound it up today." And they all listened. It was absolutely silent. "No tick," said Grandad. "Who's been fiddling with this clock?" He looked very cross. Andrew thought:

*"Oh dear, oh dear, I'm to blame,*
*The clock will never be the same."*

Everybody looked very cross. Andrew said, "I'm sorry. I touched the weight."

His grandad said, "Never mind, I can fix it." And he looked at the watch on his wrist and fixed the hands on the grandfather clock and pulled the weight so that the clock started to tick again. Slowly.

*Tick!*
*Tick!*
*Tick!*

*Then the clock went Bong! Bong! Bong!*
*and everybody shouted, "Happy New Year!"*

Then the clock made a whirring noise and

*Bong!*
*Bong!*
*Bong!*

and everybody shouted, "Happy New Year!" and kissed and hugged one another. Outside the house there was the noise of bells and car horns and ships' sirens and train whistles. Andrew ran into the hallway and rang the bell on his little red bike and everybody laughed. He said to himself:

*"I wish, I wish with all my might*
*That Hogmanay was every night."*

*Andrew McAndrew sat on his front-door step
watching a creepy crawly.*

# ANDREW McANDREW AND THE WHEELS

Andrew McAndrew sat on his front-door step watching a creepy crawly. It had so many legs – hundreds and hundreds of them like the teeth of a comb – that they rippled as it walked along. When the creepy crawly went away Andrew was bored. He said to himself:

*"I wish, I wish I'd something to do.*
*Go to Grandad. Maybe he's bored too."*

So Andrew McAndrew went to see his grandad, who was out in his shed with the squeaky door.

"Hello, Grandad," said Andrew.

"Well if it isn't Andrew," said his gran-dad. He was bending over banging and hammering at something lying on the floor.

"What do you think I'm making?"

Andrew looked and saw a board with a little seat on it. At the back and front were two metal rods. Andrew said to himself:

*"I hope, I hope with all my heart*
*Grandad is building a bogie cart."*

Then he said out loud, "I think it's a bogie cart."

"Full marks. That's what it is." Andrew jumped up and down and yelled.

"Don't get so excited, Andrew McAn-drew. It's not finished yet. What do we need to finish it?"

Andrew looked at the cart and thought of the creepy crawly.

"Something it can go on," he said. "Legs."

"Legs?" shouted his grandad.

"I mean wheels," said Andrew.

"That's better."

His grandad took him by the hand and they walked down the road to the scrap-yard. There were lots of old cars and prams and washing machines piled on top of one another. His grandad knew the man who worked in the scrap-yard. Grandad seemed to know everybody.

"The man says we can have anything we want to make our bogie cart."

Andrew and his grandad walked round the piles of rubbish. Andrew found two big wheels from an old battered pram and his grandad got two small silvery wheels from somewhere else.

They took the wheels back to Grandad's

*Andrew McAndrew tried to hide
beneath the bench.*

shed. It was cold in the shed and Grandad went off to make some hot chocolate. Andrew thought:

*"Andrew McAndrew, be a smart lad.*
*Finish the bogie for your grandad."*

So he took a big pram wheel and fitted it to one rod and fitted a small silvery wheel to the other end. And he did the same with the back rod. It didn't look right at all because the bogie cart was lopsided.

Just then his grandad came in with the hot chocolate. When he saw the bogie cart he shouted, "Who did that?"

"I did, Grandad. I'm sorry."

"The two pram wheels go at the back and the two silvery wheels go at the front." He sounded very angry. Andrew McAndrew tried to hide beneath the bench. "Don't worry. I can fix it," said his grandad, giving him his cup of hot chocolate. He fixed the bogie cart so that it was no longer lopsided. He tied a piece of rope to the axle so that Andrew could steer to the left or to the right by pulling it. When they pulled it out of the shed the wheels sounded very squeaky.

"That's an awful noise," said his grandad. "What it needs is a drop of oil." He got his oil can with the long thin spout and squeezed it into the noisy part of the wheels. The oil can made a clicking sound and the oil came out. Andrew spun the wheels and this time there was no squeaking.

"It's ready for the road," said his grandad. Andrew McAndrew got into the seat and his grandad puffed and puffed as he pushed the cart to the top of the hill.

"I'm too old for this," he said and he stood up and put his hand to his back. But Andrew was away. Steering the wheels with the rope he said a little rhyme to himself.

*"Andrew McAndrew, how great it feels*
*To be whizzing down a hill on wheels!"*

*"Hello, Grandad,"* said Andrew and jumped
up and down with wee tight jumps.

# ANDREW McANDREW
## AND THE
## CALENDAR

It was the day before Andrew McAndrew's birthday. Today he was only four but tomorrow he would be five.

Andrew loved to visit his grandad because every time he did, his grandad had something good to show him.

"Hello, Andrew McAndrew," said his grandad. He was unwrapping a brown paper parcel.

"Hello, Grandad," said Andrew and jumped up and down with wee tight jumps waiting to see what was in it.

"This is a present I got from a friend of mine." He opened the parcel and showed Andrew a little black box with windows.

"What is it?" said Andrew.

"It's a calendar. For telling the date. In the first little window, look here, what does it say?"

"I don't know. I can't read yet," said Andrew.

"Oh, I forgot. Well it says the day of the week. Look. Monday. And if you turn this wee knob here it changes to Tuesday and then Wednesday. And in the next little window it tells you the date. Now it says the ninth and if you turn this little knob here it changes to the tenth."

"Oh, it's great," said Andrew as all the numbers turned.

"But it's not finished yet," said his grandad. "The biggest window of all tells you the month of the year. January. Turn the knob. February. Turn it again for March. What do you think of that, Andrew

McAndrew?" Andrew stood looking at the calendar box with his eyes wide. "Isn't it wonderful, the works of a wheelbarrow, eh? Now let's get today's date fixed!"

As Andrew's grandad fiddled with the knobs Andrew McAndrew made a wish.

*"Andrew McAndrew, wouldn't it be great*
*If a wee boy like me could fix the date."*

"There," said his grandad, "Wednesday the eighth of February," and he set the calendar on the sideboard. "Well, Andrew, how would you like a glass of lemonade?"

Andrew said, "Yes," and his grandad went to the kitchen to get it for him. Andrew looked at the calendar and said:

*"Andrew McAndrew, there's a wee job,*
*Change the date by turning the knob."*

*That night Andrew McAndrew couldn't
sleep because he was so excited about his birthday.*

And he reached up to where the calendar stood on the sideboard and turned the knob backwards a bit and, *click*, the date changed. He did the same with the day of the week, *click*, and it changed too.

"Oh no!" he thought, "I've done it again."

Then his grandad came back from the kitchen with the lemonade and Andrew kept quiet and drank it.

That night Andrew McAndrew couldn't sleep because he was so excited about his birthday. As he lay in bed in his best pyjamas he thought:

*"I wish, I wish, with all my might,*
*My birthday would begin tonight."*

When his mum and dad were going to bed they looked in at him and saw that

Andrew was still awake. They brought him downstairs for some hot chocolate to make him sleep.

"Do you know what time it is, Andrew?" said his mum.

"No."

"It's twelve o'clock."

Then his dad did a funny thing. He began to sing.

"Happy birthday to you, happy birthday to you, happy birthday, dear Andrew, happy birthday to you."

"But my birthday is tomorrow," said Andrew.

"After twelve o'clock *is* tomorrow," said his dad laughing.

"Can I have my presents then?"

"No," said his mum. "Wait until morning."

So when he had finished his chocolate

*Then his dad did a funny thing.*
*He began to sing.*

*They wore paper hats
and blew squeakers.*

right down to the sandy bit at the bottom of the cup, Andrew went to bed. In the morning his mum and dad gave him his presents. He got a book and a pair of socks and a toy watch. He played with the toy watch all morning, counting the hours until his friends came to his party. They wore paper hats and blew squeakers and ate egg sandwiches and banana sandwiches and cake and crisps.

But after the party Andrew began to feel sad. His grandad had not brought him a present. He always brought him a present on his birthday. After tea Andrew had his bath and put on his best pyjamas and his mum read him a story out of his new book. But he wasn't listening. He was thinking.

*"Indeed, indeed, it's most unpleasant*
*When Grandad doesn't bring a present."*

His mum tucked him in and went downstairs. Then Andrew heard the front door opening and his grandad's voice. He tiptoed out of bed and listened. His grandad said, "Here's Andrew McAndrew's present for his birthday tomorrow."

"But it was today," said his mother.

"I must have got the date wrong," said his grandad.

Then Andrew remembered all about the knobs on the calendar thing and he ran and hid under the bedclothes. His grandad stamped up the stairs and into the room.

"Who was fiddling with my calendar?" He sounded very angry.

"It was me, Grandad," said Andrew from beneath the bedclothes. "I'm sorry."

"Never mind. I can fix it to the right date when I get home. It just means that your birthday present is a little late."

His grandad took out a little parcel from his pocket and gave it to Andrew. Andrew unwrapped it as quickly as he could. It was a mouth organ. Andrew McAndrew could play only one tune and he tried it out sitting up in bed.

*Dah-dah, dee-dee, dum, dah!*

"What's that tune?" asked his grandad.
"Happy birthday to me," said Andrew and they both laughed.

THE

END